SCOOBY-DOO!

AND THE

HAUNTED
CASTLE

D0774696

working in partnership with National Literacy Trust

SCHOLASTIC

Published in the UK by Scholastic Children's Books, 2020
Euston House, 24 Eversholt Street, London, NW1 1DB
A division of Scholastic Limited

London ~ New York ~ Toronto ~ Sydney ~ Auckland
Mexico City ~ New Delhi ~ Hong Kong

SCHOLASTIC and associated logos are trademarks and/or
registered trademarks of Scholastic Inc.

Made for McDonald's 2020

The following trade marks are owned by McDonald's Corporation and its affiliates: McDonald's,
Happy Readers and the Golden Arches Logo. © 2020 McDonald's

Copyright © 2020 Hanna-Barbera.
SCOOBY-DOO and all related characters and elements
are trademarks of and © Hanna-Barbera.
WB SHIELD: ™ & © Warner Bros. Entertainment Inc. (s20)

The National Literacy Trust is a registered charity no. 1116260 and a company limited by guarantee no. 5836486
registered in England and Wales and a registered charity in Scotland no. SC042944. Registered address: 68
South Lambeth Road, London SW8 1RL. National Literacy Trust logo and reading tips copyright © National
Literacy Trust, 2020 literacytrust.org.uk

ISBN 978 07023 0291 6

A CIP catalogue record for this book is available from the British Library.

All rights reserved.
This book is sold subject to the condition that it shall not, by way of trade or otherwise, be lent, hired out or
otherwise circulated in any form of binding or cover other than that in which it is published. No part of this
publication may be reproduced, stored in a retrieval system, or transmitted in any form or by any other means
(electronic, mechanical, photocopying, recording or otherwise) without prior written
permission of Scholastic Limited.

Printed in China
TSHQ 926

1 3 5 7 9 10 8 6 4 2

www.scholastic.co.uk

CHAPTER 1

BOOM! The thunder rumbled through the dark, stormy night.

"Yikes! What was that?" asked Shaggy from the back of the Mystery Machine.

"Just a little thunder, Shaggy. Nothing to worry about," Daphne said from the front seat.

"Nothing to worry about? Didja hear that, Scoob? The sky's gonna come crashing down on us and there's nothing to worry about."

"Come on, Shaggy," Fred called from the driver's seat. "We'll make it to the cinema just fine. It's only a little storm."

"I hope you're right, man, 'cause I'm getting hungry. How 'bout you, Scooby-Doo?"

"Rou bet!" Scooby said, excitedly.

The Mystery Machine carefully made its way along the winding roads. It was raining hard, but the cinema was just a few miles away.

"Jinkies," Velma said. "Fred, maybe this wasn't such a great shortcut."

"Yeah, it's really dark," Daphne added. "Can you see the road?"

"I can see it just fine," said Fred. *BANG!*

The Mystery Machine hit a huge bump and skidded off the road.

"The sky is falling!" Shaggy yelled.

"Rold me, Raggy!" Scooby yelped.

The van came to a stop.

"Is everyone okay?" Fred asked.

"I'm fine," Daphne said. "Velma?"

"I'm okay, thanks. Good thing I was wearing my seat belt!"

Fred turned towards the back of the van. "How about you guys?"

Shaggy and Scooby were nowhere to be seen.

"Shaggy? Scooby?" Velma called.

"We're fine," came Shaggy's voice from under the back seat. "We're just, like, uh, checking to make sure the floor's okay."

"Hmmm . . ." Daphne said. "I wonder what happened."

"Judging by the sound, I'll bet it's a flat," Velma said.

"I'll check it out," Fred said. He grabbed a torch from the glove box and went out to look at the tyres.

"You can come out now," Velma said. "I'm sure the floor is fine."

"You can never be too sure, right, Scoob?" Shaggy said.

"Right!" Scooby barked.

Fred got back into the van. "It's a flat, all right. We must've hit a rock or something back there. Everyone sit tight. We'll be on our way to the cinema before you know it. Shaggy, give me a hand with the spare."

"Uh, no can do, Freddy-o," Shaggy said.

"Why not?" Fred asked. "Don't tell me you're still scared."

"I'm not scared," Shaggy replied.

BOOOOOM!

"Yikes! The sky's falling again!"
Shaggy yelled. He jumped into
Scooby's arms. Scooby laughed.
Velma, Daphne and Fred did, too.

"Like, what's so funny?"

Scooby looked
at Shaggy and said,
"BOOOOOM!"
Everyone started
laughing again.

"Very funny, Scoob," Shaggy said.

"Enough kidding around," Fred
said. "Let's get this tyre changed."

"Like I said before, Fred, no can
do. There's no spare."

"No spare?" Fred, Daphne, and Velma all looked at Shaggy and Scooby. "Why not?"

"Like, Scooby and I needed room for our survival kit. It contains everything we need to survive an emergency. Right, Scooby?"

Scooby nodded.

"I'm afraid to see this survival kit," Daphne said to the gang.

"I have a pretty good hunch what's inside," Velma added.

Shaggy opened the spare tyre compartment. Inside were grapes, apples and bananas.

"Well, gang, we're stuck with a flat and no spare tyre," Fred said.

"Sounds like an emergency situation to me," Shaggy said.

"Me roo!" Scooby agreed. The two of them reached for some snacks and started eating.

"Hey! What's that?" Daphne said. She pointed through the windscreen. Lightning flashed across the sky and lit up the outline of a huge castle just up the road. "It looks like a house," she said.

"More of a mansion," Fred added.

"More like a castle," Velma said.

"More like a haunted castle, if you ask me," Shaggy said.

"There's only one thing to do," Fred said. "Let's go and get help."

"Then maybe we can still make the cinema," Velma said.

Shaggy and Scooby didn't budge.

"Aren't you coming, boys?" Daphne asked.

"No, thank you," Shaggy said. "Going to a scary castle on a stormy night spells nothing but trouble."

"Nothing but rouble!" Scooby echoed.

"You're being ridiculous. That castle isn't haunted," Velma said.

Shaggy took a bite out his apple.

"We'll be fine right here."

"Suit yourself," Fred said.

Shaggy and Scooby watched their friends get out of the van. Velma led the way, shining the torch through the storm.

"They're outside in the pouring rain. We're inside a dry van with our emergency survival kit. Who's ridiculous now, huh, Scooby?"

FLASH! CRASH! BOOM! Shaggy

and Scooby watched a lightning
bolt strike a tree next to the Mystery
Machine. The tree crashed to
the ground. The whole Mystery
Machine shook. Shaggy and Scooby
looked at each other.

"WAIT FOR US!"
They jumped out of the van and
raced toward the castle.

CHAPTER 2

Shaggy and Scooby ran up the winding driveway toward Montgomery Castle. The road was very steep, and the rain didn't make

the climb any easier. Finally, Shaggy
and Scooby arrived at the front door
out of breath.

"So, like, I wonder where Fred
and the girls are," Shaggy said.

"Boo!"

Shaggy and Scooby screamed.

It was only Fred.
He was standing there
with Daphne and
Velma. "We thought
that was you running
past us," Fred laughed.

"So, Shaggy," Daphne said, "why
did you leave the safety of the van?"

"Like, the van wasn't so safe anymore," Shaggy said.

"Rim-ber!" Scooby yelled. He fell over like a tree into Shaggy's arms.

"Enough clowning around. We're here to use the phone," Fred said. He reached for the door knocker. "I just hope somebody's home," he added.

"Judging by the lights up there, I'd say there's a good chance," Velma offered. She pointed to the large windows on the second floor.

The door slowly creaked open. The gang looked inside but couldn't see a thing. Then, out of the darkness, a the face of an elderly man appeared. The candle he was holding gave him an eerie glow.

"Uh, Scooby-Doo and I just remembered we forgot to do something," Shaggy said.

"What's that?" asked Daphne.

"Stay in the van!" Shaggy replied.

"Please," the man said. He placed his wrinkled hand on Shaggy's shoulder. "Please, come in."

Shaggy gulped. "Nothing to be afraid of, Scooby," Shaggy said. "You go first." He gave Scooby a push. The gang followed Scooby into the dark front hall. The door closed behind them with a slam.

"My name is Chives," the elderly man said.

"Pardon me," Fred said, "but our van has a flat tyre out in front of your house and—"

"Well, Chives, who's here?" asked a voice. Another man approached. He was also carrying a candle. "The name's Clifton Montgomery. This is my butler, Chives. Frightful night, isn't it?"

"Yes, it is, Mr Montgomery," Fred replied.

"Please, call me Clift. Do come in and dry off," he continued. "I'm so sorry about the lights. The fixture is under repair and we never got around to putting any candles here."

"Excuse me, Mr Montgomery, but—" Fred started to say.

"Uh-uh-uh-call me Clift."

"Okay, Clift. Can we use your phone? Our van out front has a flat and we don't have a spare." Fred glared at Shaggy and Scooby.

"So sorry, but the phone lines are down. Chives will take care of it once the storm passes. Now please, join us for dinner."

"That's very generous, but—" Velma began.

"I won't take no for an answer," interrupted Clift.

Shaggy and Scooby looked at each other. "You heard the man. He won't take no for an answer. Maybe this place isn't so bad, after all," Shaggy said.

Chives led the way out of the

front hall and up a huge, curving staircase. As the gang made their way up, Scooby and Shaggy sniffed the air. Their keen sense of smell caught a whiff of fresh roast beef.

"Like I said before, Scooby-Doo," Shaggy said, "there's nothing to be afraid of here."

CHAPTER 3

At the top of the stairs, the gang found themselves in the Great Hall. It was the largest room they had ever seen. Everything about it was big. The walls towered above and were made of huge blocks of stone. Old shields, swords and other medieval tools covered one wall. A row of ten suits of armour, each seven feet tall, lined another wall. Above, they noticed three giant candelabras glowing with the light of a hundred candles.

"Jinkies, who's that?" Velma asked. She pointed to a painting of a very stern-looking man.

"That's Ward Montgomery, my great-great-grandfather," Clift said.

"Amazing," Daphne said.

"Wow," Fred added.

"So, like, when do we eat?" asked Shaggy. Chives walked up behind Shaggy. "Right this way, sir," he said.

Shaggy jumped. "Like, don't sneak up on us like that, man," Shaggy said. "You almost scared poor Scooby to death. You okay, Scoob? Scoob?" Shaggy looked around but Scooby wasn't there.

Scooby was already following the aroma of roast beef.

"Your dog would make a fine bloodhound," Clift said. "He's already found his way to the dining room. Shall we?" Clift motioned for everyone to follow Scooby-Doo.

The dining room was brightly lit by several electric chandeliers. There were already a few people sitting around the long table, but Shaggy and Scooby-Doo didn't notice the people. They were looking at all the food.

"Now this is what I call a dinner

table," Shaggy said in awe. Down the centre of the long table was a row of silver platters. Each platter was piled high with food.

"Do you see what I see, Scooby?" Shaggy asked.

"Rou bet," Scooby replied.

The two of them walked over to the table. Never before had they seen so much food. There was roast beef, chicken, fish, vegetables of all kinds, long breads, skinny breads, round breads and platters with mounds of spaghetti.

"Please, please, have a seat

anywhere," Clift said. He waved his hand and pointed to some empty chairs. The gang sat down around the table.

"I have some very exciting news to share," Clift said from the head of the table. "But before I start, let's take a moment to introduce ourselves. It's so much nicer eating with friends than strangers."

"Really, Clift, is this another of your silly games?" asked the woman sitting next to him.

Fred shrugged and said, "I guess I'll start. I'm Fred, and this is Daphne, Velma, Shaggy and Scooby-Doo. Our van has a flat just outside the castle. We only came in to use the phone."

"And I forced them to join us for dinner. The more the merrier, I always say. Barbara, your turn."

"I'm Barbara Redding," said the woman sitting next to Clift. "You probably know that I'm the mayor of this town. And I've been trying to convince Clift to donate the castle to the town as a museum."

The old man next to Velma leaned forward in his chair and

coughed. "Sonny DiPesto. Estate sales, shopping centres, car parks. I've been after this place for years for a medieval-themed amusement park. I want to call it Knightland."

The woman with red hair across from him shook her head disapprovingly.

"I'm Sally MacIntyre, from Scotland's Royal Museum. We want to get this castle returned to Scotland where it belongs."

Clift stood beside his chair at the head of the table. "Now, some of you may not know the rich history of the Montgomery family. How my great-great-grandfather, Ward Montgomery, brought this castle over from Scotland stone by stone. The Montgomery family has lived here for years. And as you may know, I have no family of my own. Therefore, as of midnight tonight,

I am turning the castle over to the people of our town for use as a museum and park."

Mayor Redding exclaimed, "How wonderful!"

Sonny DiPesto reached for his glass of water. "We'll see how long a museum lasts in this town."

"Ah, 'tis a sad day for the folks back in Scotland," said Sally.

"A toast to Clifton Montgomery," Mayor Redding said. Everyone raised

their glasses.

"I love a good toast," Shaggy said, "especially with butter and jam."

"Rike ris!" Scooby took a huge bite of bread and smiled.

"Hip, hip, hooray!" everyone cheered. "Hip, hip, hooray!"

Suddenly, the lights went out.

CHAPTER 4

"Like, where is everybody?" Shaggy asked.

"Everyone stay calm," Clift called. "Just a power failure. Chives will get some candles. Chives!"

Someone lit a match. A candle

moved slowly through the darkness and illuminated a ghostly face.

"It looks like Ward Montgomery!" Velma cried.

The ghost's face was pale. His skin looked wrinkled and saggy. There was no mistaking it. It was Ward Montgomery!

"Like, I told you guys this place was haunted!" Shaggy said.

The ghost began to speak in a scratchy voice. "Montgomery Castle must remain in our family. I curse every stone in this castle and anyone who dares to remain here after midnight. Leave this place now and never return. Let what happens to my great-great-grandson be your only warning."

The ghost blew out the candle.

Clift screamed. Then there was the sound of a door slamming.

"What's going on?" Mayor Redding yelled.

A moment later, the lights came back on. Clift was gone. Everyone called for him but he did not answer. Shaggy looked over and saw that Scooby-Doo was also gone.

"Oh, no! The ghost got Scooby-Doo, too. Scoob? Scooby-Doo, where are you?" he called.

"Runder rere," Scooby's voice came from under the table.

Shaggy lifted the tablecloth. There was Scooby with a plate of spaghetti in front of him.

"That's the spirit, Scooby. No sense being scared on an empty stomach." Shaggy said, joining him under the table.

"Sonny," Mayor Redding said, "what are you doing over there?"

Sonny was standing by the grandfather clock, holding a candle. "After the ghost blew out the candle, I heard sounds from over here," Sonny explained. "I moved as fast as I could, but by the time I got here, all I found was this candle."

"We'd better get some help," the mayor decided. "We'll have to drive back to town." Mayor Redding, Sonny DiPesto and Sally MacIntyre headed back to the Great Hall. Fred, Velma and Daphne followed them.

As everyone was passing through the hall, they heard knocking come from a huge trunk. They all froze.

"Help!" came a voice from inside.

It wasn't Clift's voice. Fred, Velma and Daphne ran to open the trunk.

"Chives?" Sonny DiPesto said.

"I was on my way to check the phones when the lights went out," Chives explained as he got out of the trunk. "I tripped and fell into the trunk. The lid got stuck."

Mayor Redding said, "Thank goodness that ghost didn't get you, too." She turned to Fred, Daphne and Velma. "Would you like a lift?"

"No, thanks," Fred answered. "We, uh, have to, uh—"

"Find our friends," said Daphne.

"I wouldn't stay too long," Sally MacIntyre warned. "In Scotland, we take our ghosts very seriously. I advise you to do the same."

"We'll be fine," Velma told them.

"I'll be sure to send a tow truck, then," Mayor Redding said.

"Goodnight." She, Sonny and Sally started down the huge staircase.

Chives turned to Fred, Daphne and Velma. "You should leave this place," he warned. "That ghost means business. I'm not going to let what happened to Master Clift happen to me." Chives turned and hurried down the stairs. A moment later, the front door slammed shut.

Shaggy and Scooby then joined Fred, Daphne and Velma in the Great Hall.

"Like, where did everyone go?" Shaggy asked.

"They went for help," said Velma.

"Sounds like a good plan to me," Shaggy said.

"I have a better idea," Fred said.

Velma nodded. "Let's get to the bottom of this."

"I was afraid you were going to say that," Shaggy moaned.

CHAPTER 5

"Let's split up, gang," Fred said. "Velma, you, Shaggy and Scooby look around here in the Great Hall. Daphne and I will check out the dining room."

"Like, Scooby and I could check the dining room while you three look here," Shaggy volunteered.

Scooby nodded his head.

"Reah, reah, reah."

"Come on, you two," Velma said. "The quicker we get started, the quicker we can finish." Fred and Daphne went back into the dining room. Velma pointed towards the suits of armour.

"You two look over there. I'll look around here."

Shaggy and Scooby walked over to one of the suits of armour.

"Like, how'd anybody get out of these things?" Shaggy asked.

"Ran ropener!" Scooby said.

"Can opener? That's funny, Scooby-Doo!" They both laughed.

Across the room, Velma was looking at the weapons hanging on the wall. She reached up and touched a shield. In the middle of the shield was a lion. It was solid gold with large emerald eyes. Its front paws were raised to attack.

"Must be the Montgomery family crest," she said to herself. Velma traced the design of the lion. Then she noticed something. The lion's claws were made of silver and stuck out. She touched the claws. Suddenly, a doorway opened in the middle of the stone wall.

"Jinkies," Velma whispered. "It's a secret passage." She took a torch from her pocket. She turned it on and went into the passage. The secret door closed behind her.

Meanwhile, Shaggy was putting on one of the metal helmets. He picked up a sword and posed like a knight. "Hey, look at me, Scooby. I'm Sir Loin of Beef! Get it? Sir Loin? Sirloin?" He and Scooby laughed. "You can be Sir Scoobalot."

"Rooby-Dooby-Doobalot!" Scooby sang.

"And we must duel to the death for the last piece of roast beef," Shaggy added. "Take that!" Shaggy

lunged at Scooby. Scooby grabbed
a sword from one of the knights.
He lunged at Shaggy, but Shaggy
jumped back and ran after him.

"Ruh-roh," Scooby said. He
giggled as he weaved around the
suits of armour.

"I'll get you, Sir Scoobalot!" Shaggy called as he chased Scooby around the knights.

Scooby looked up and saw the ghost of Ward Montgomery standing behind Shaggy. "Rikes! The rhost! The rhost!" Scooby warned.

"That's right," Shaggy said. "This is about the roast. And the last piece of the roast is mine. So, what do you have to say about that?"

"Rerind rou!"

"The roast is behind me?" Shaggy said. Scooby nodded quickly. Shaggy slowly turned around and looked over his shoulder. He saw the ghost. "Yikes!" he yelled.

"The rhost! The rhost!" both he and Scooby screamed.

Shaggy and Scooby ran through the ghost's legs. "This way, Scoob!" Shaggy called. He ran around and around the suits of armour. Scooby followed. So did the ghost. "Faster, Scooby!" The two ducked behind the last suit of armour.

The ghost of Ward Montgomery stood in the middle of the hall. He couldn't see Shaggy and Scooby.

"You know, Scoob," Shaggy panted, "that ghost is more out of breath than we are!"

Scooby tried to get a better look. As he peeked around, he hit the suit of armour. With a slow creak, it fell onto the suit of armour next to it.

CRASH!

And then – CRASH! CRASH! CRASH! All the suits of armour fell like dominoes. The ghost whipped around and saw Scooby and Shaggy.

"Quick, Scooby-Doo – in here!" Shaggy jumped into the trunk behind them. Scooby followed and slammed the lid.

The ghost ran over to the trunk and locked it.

"I don't like the sound of that," Shaggy said. "Help!" he shouted.

"Relp!" Scooby shouted. They pounded on the trunk.

"Velma! Fred! Daphne! Anyone!"

CHAPTER 6

Scooby and Shaggy were still in the trunk. "I guess we're goners," said Shaggy. "The ghost must've got Velma, Fred and Daphne by now. I told them this place was bad news."

Suddenly, they heard footsteps.

"Oh, no, it's the ghost!" Shaggy exclaimed. "Goodbye, Scoob."

"Rood-rye, Raggy."

They heard a click and shut their eyes. The lid opened, and Shaggy cracked open his right eye just a bit.

"Fred! Daphne! Boy, are we glad to see you!"

The two of them jumped out of the trunk. Shaggy hugged Fred. Scooby hugged Daphne. Shaggy hugged Daphne. Scooby hugged Fred. Shaggy hugged Scooby.

"Knock it off, you two," Fred said sternly. "Have you seen Velma?"

"Like, we thought she was with you," Shaggy answered.

"And we thought she was still with you," Daphne replied.

"This is getting creepy, man," said Shaggy. "First Clift. Now Velma. I told you this place was bad news."

"Rad news!" Scooby echoed.

"Hey! Where is everybody?" It was Velma's voice. And it was coming from the dining room.

The gang ran into the dining room. There was Velma, sitting in Clift's seat at the head of the table.

"There you are," she said.

"Are you all right?" said Daphne.

"Jinkies," Velma replied. "I'm great. And I found some things that will help us solve this mystery."

"Like, like what?" asked Shaggy.

"For starters, wouldn't you like to know where I've been?" she asked.

"We were just trying to figure that out," Fred said.

"While Shaggy and Scooby were playing knights of the kitchen table," Velma recounted, "I was on the other side of the Great Hall. I noticed the Montgomery family shield on the wall. I discovered a switch that opened a hidden door."

"A secret passage!" Fred gasped.

"Not just one," Velma added. "A whole bunch of secret walkways.

They go all over the castle."

"Walkways that make it easy
for a ghost to get around quickly,"
Daphne added.

"But only if the ghost knows his
way around," Velma replied.

"I'll tell you one thing about that ghost," Shaggy said. "He may be able to get around quickly, but he's a little out of shape."

"What are you talking about, Shaggy?" Daphne asked.

"I've never seen a ghost out of breath before," Shaggy replied.

Velma and Fred looked at each other and nodded.

"I've got a good idea just who our ghost really is," Velma said.

"If you're thinking what I'm thinking," Fred said, "it's time to set a trap."

CHAPTER 7

The gang huddled together at the head of the dinner table. "Okay, everyone, listen up. Here's the plan," Fred began. "We know we have a ghost who wants everyone out of the castle. But why?"

"So he can eat all this food himself?" Shaggy suggested, looking at the table still set for dinner.

"Actually, Shaggy, you're not that far off," Velma replied. "There's clearly something in this castle that the ghost wants for himself."

"Right," Fred said. "So we're going to get this ghost to show himself by pretending we're not going anywhere. But that won't be enough, so we'll have to scare him. So, how do you scare a ghost?"

"Sneak up behind him and yell, 'Boo!'" Daphne said.

"Exactly," Velma replied.

"But where are we going to get another ghost?" Shaggy asked.

Everyone then turned to Scooby.

"Ruh?" Scooby said.

"Come on, Scooby-Doo, there's nothing to it," Fred said. "We'll dress you up. All you'll have to do is say 'boo' when the ghost appears."

"Ruh-uh," Scooby said, shaking his head.

"Please, Scooby?" Daphne asked.

"Roh way." He sat

down and crossed his paws.

"Not even for a Scooby snack?" Velma asked.

Scooby did not even blink. "Nope."

"Even for two Scooby snacks?"

Scooby's stomach growled. His right ear twitched a little. But he sat firm. "Ruh-ruh."

"Three Scooby snacks?"

Scooby could not take it any longer. He jumped up and nodded eagerly. "Rokay, rokay, rokay!"

Velma took three Scooby snacks out of her pocket. She threw them to Scooby one at a time.

"Daphne, you and Velma sit at the table and pretend to be eating dinner," Fred said.

"Like, why can't I sit at the table and pretend to be eating?" Shaggy asked. "I'm much better at eating than catching ghosts."

"Shaggy, you help Scooby into his costume. Then stand behind the grandfather clock. Scooby will hide behind this curtain and I'll be next to him. When Scooby scares the ghost, grab the tablecloth. I'll help you capture the ghost."

"If you say so," Shaggy said. He

helped Scooby into some armour. Daphne and Velma took their places at the table. Scooby hid behind the curtain hanging on the wall. Fred stood in front of the curtain. Shaggy stood next to the grandfather clock on the opposite wall.

"Boy, am I glad we decided to stay the night," Daphne said.

"Yeah," Velma added. "No ghost is going to scare me."

"Especially one as harmless as Ward Montgomery," said Daphne.

They helped themselves to some food. Suddenly, the lights went out.

When they came back on, the ghost of Ward Montgomery was there.

"I warned you people to leave before midnight. Now it is too late. This castle and everyone in it are cursed for all time."

Fred nodded at Scooby.

Scooby gulped and cleared his throat. He jumped out and yelled, "Rooby-Dooby-BOOOOOOOOO!"

The ghost turned around. He saw Scooby and leaped back.

"Now, Shaggy!" Fred yelled.

Shaggy jumped out, grabbed the tablecloth and gave it a quick

tug. *Whoosh!* The cloth flew out from under the plates. He and Fred threw it over the ghost. Daphne and Velma pushed the ghost into a chair.

"You are all cursed!" the ghost yelled from under the tablecloth.

The next thing they heard was pounding coming from the walls.

"It's a real ghost!" Shaggy yelled.

Scooby-Doo jumped out of his armour and dived under the table.

"So much for can openers, eh, Scoob?" Shaggy said. "Save some space for me!" He dived under the table after Scooby.

CHAPTER 8

"**D**on't be silly," Velma said. "There's no ghost!" She walked up to the grandfather clock. She ran her fingers over it and pushed a button. A doorway opened. Out came Clifton Montgomery. His hands were tied. There was tape on his mouth. He had a bump on his forehead. But aside from all that, he seemed fine.

"Clift!" Daphne said. "Are you all right?"

She slowly removed the tape from his mouth.

"Frightfully woozy, but otherwise fine, thanks," he said.

Fred kept an eye on the ghost while Velma and Daphne untied Clift. Clift sat down and gently felt his forehead.

"What a bump!" Velma said.

"Yes, indeed," Clift said. He reached for a glass of water.

"Do you know what happened?" Velma asked.

"I remember telling everyone the news about the castle. The lights went out and the ghost appeared. Next thing I know, I'm tucked away in a tiny cupboard somewhere."

Daphne pointed under the table. "Speaking of being tucked away," she said.

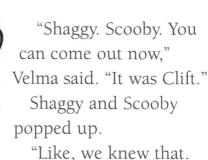

"Shaggy. Scooby. You can come out now," Velma said. "It was Clift."

Shaggy and Scooby popped up.

"Like, we knew that. We were just, uh—"

"You were just making sure the floor was okay?" Daphne asked.

Suddenly, there was another strange knock. Everyone froze.

"Not another ghost," Shaggy moaned.

"Just the front door," Clift said. They heard the door open and voices in the hallway.

"Hello? Anyone here?"

"In here," Clift called.

Mayor Redding entered the room with some police officers.

"Clift! Thank goodness you're okay. Sorry it took so long, but the storm caused trouble on the roads."

"How about we see if this ghost is who we think it is?" Fred asked.

"Great idea," Clift agreed.

Fred took the tablecloth off the ghost's head. "Would you like to do the honours, Clift?" Fred asked.

"Love to." Clift lifted off the

ghost's mask and gasped. "Chives!"
he shouted. "But why?"

Chives looked sadly at Clift.
"Because this is my home. I wanted
to scare everyone off so I wouldn't
have to leave. I've been here most of
my life. And unlike you, sir, I don't
have other places to live. Without
the castle, I'd be without a home."
Tear filled his eyes.

"Oh, Clift," Mayor Redding said, "you really can't blame dear Chives. Do you have to press charges?"

Velma stepped up. "Excuse me, Mr Montgomery," she said, "but before you decide, maybe you should ask him about the treasure."

"Treasure?" Shaggy asked.

"Yes, the Montgomery family treasure," Clift responded. "But how did you know about it?"

"I did some exploring through the secret passageways," Velma said.

"Good show, Velma," Clift said. "I guess you found the treasure chest."

"I did," Velma answered proudly.

"Well, Chives, what do you have to say now?" Clift asked.

Chives looked up at the police and then at Clift.

"It's true. I wanted the treasure. I figured it was the least you could do for me after all these years of service. I didn't care what happened to this place. I just needed enough time to get the treasure packed away so I could leave the country."

Clift turned to Fred, Daphne and Velma. "Why did you suspect Chives?" he asked.

Fred spoke first. "At first we suspected Mr DiPesto. When the lights came back on, he was holding the ghost's candle."

"But he couldn't have done it," Daphne added. "He was sitting next to me the whole time."

"It was after we found Chives in the trunk that things began to make sense," Velma said. "He said he tripped in the dark and got stuck."

"But the trunk is in the Great Hall," Fred continued. "And that room is lit by candles, not electricity. When the lights went out in the dining room, the candles stayed lit in the Great Hall.

Chives was the only one not with us when the ghost appeared."

"He's also lived here a long time," Daphne added. "And probably knows all the secret passages."

"But it was Shaggy and Scooby who confirmed it," Velma said. "After the ghost chased them around the Great Hall, they said he was out of breath."

"Real ghosts don't get tired out," Fred explained. "But old men do."

Chives looked up. "I would have gotten away with it if it weren't for those kids and their pesky dog."

"Take this man away, officers,"
Mayor Redding said. "The tow truck
will be here soon," she said to the
gang. "Thank you all for solving this
mystery. Goodbye, Clift, and thanks
again for your gift. I'll call tomorrow."

"You're welcome, Mayor."

The mayor left with the police officers and Chives.

Clift turned to the gang. "I am very grateful to all of you. Until your van is fixed, why don't we go ahead and have that supper?"

"What do you say, gang?" Fred asked.

"I thought you'd never ask," Shaggy said happily.

"Jeepers, that sounds just perfect, Clift," Daphne exclaimed.

"And for you," Clift said to Scooby-Doo, "I have a special treat."

Clift walked over to the table. He reached for a silver dome and lifted the lid with a flourish. "The last piece of roast beef!" he announced.

"Scooby-Dooby-Doobalot!" Scooby shouted. Everyone laughed as they sat down to eat.

HAUNTED CASTLE!

The gang have got a mystery to solve in the creepy haunted house! Beware, there are spooks, monsters and traps behind every corner! Use your stickers to make the scene even creepier!

ABOUT THE AUTHOR

As a boy, James Gelsey used to run home from school to watch the Scooby-Doo cartoons on television (only after finishing his homework). Today, he still enjoys watching them with his wife and daughter. He also has a real dog named Scooby who loves nothing more than a good Scooby Snack!